I0566449

For all the queer summer hook ups we don't remember ;)

A QUEER SUMMER NIGHT IN COWTOWN
10 hot and cold queer shorts for the 10 days
of the Greatest Outdoor Show on Earth
by YYC Queer Writers
curated by M. Jane Colette

Published in collaboration with M. Jane Colette
& YYC Queer Writers by
GENRES were made to be BROKEN
121, 104-1240 Kensington Rd NW
Calgary, Alberta T2N3P7 Canada

ISBN: 978-1-989297-05-6 (trade paperback)
ISBN: 978-1-989297-06-3 (ebook)

www.mjanecolette.com/YYCQueerWriters

CONTENTS

On the Floor by Alyssa Linn Palmer 1
Voyeur by Dirk Van Dyk 7
On the Range by Dallas Barnes 11
Coming by PW Zellie 17
The Steward of the Treaty 7 Sodium Forest
by Beatrice Aucoin 19
Hawk's Eye by Karen O. 26
After Care by T 31
First Rodeo by Lotis Cervantes 33
You, and the Herds by Callan Field 42
Dhakira by M. Jane Colette 46
About YYC Queer Writers 53
More Projects 54

ON THE FLOOR

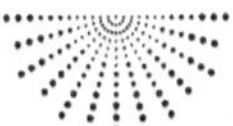

BY ALYSSA LINN PALMER

Those boots. Oh my lord, those boots.

I spot them on a woman sitting on the Skyride above me, cruising towards the far end of the Stampede grounds. And of course, I notice those gorgeous legs, olive-toned skin glossy in the setting sun. I'm not sure which sight is better, the boots or the legs. I suppose it doesn't matter. Put together, they knock me out.

And I'm just close enough to the end of the ride that I can casually hang about. It'll be a better use of my time than pacing through the grounds, being bored. I've never been a fan of Stampede, but after multiple nights of being woken up by fireworks, I've bitten the bullet. I'll eat some junk food—though the scorpions on pizza are a definite no—and play a few games, win a few toys if I'm lucky, then go back to my condo and crash with exhaustion. And maybe even watch some fireworks instead of cursing them.

The woman gets off the ride and turns to stroll near

me, then pauses. I meet her gaze, and she meets mine. I'm not trying to be creepy, but I feel something. Interest. Intrigue. Her gaze holds mine a beat longer and I feel my face flush. I glance down at her boots again. I'm pretty sure they're Fluevogs. They have that look, that certain something about them.

She looks lost. She's glancing around, back and forth, squinting a bit in the sun, which is just at that angle where it's blinding. She needs a hat. Or shades. I've been sensible about it, wearing a light, long-sleeved top, jeans, boots and shades, topped off with a slightly battered cowboy hat that I found stuffed in my closet. She's in a jean-skirt, a little too short, and a snug tank top, her dark hair spilling over her shoulders. It suits her, shows her curves, her striking self. But she is going to regret it and soon. Sunburn sucks. This sun is unforgiving.

I feel bad for her. And I feel hot for her, all at once.

She walks slowly by, and as she passes me, I say "Love those boots" in a friendly yet loudish voice. She stops, turns, smiles at me. I'm struck dumb. All my dreams come true at once.

"Thanks. You haven't seen a couple of guys round here, have you? Tall, dark hair, a bit larger?"

Disappointment.

I shake my head.

"Damn." She pulls a phone out of her back pocket and thumbs it, looking at something. "They were supposed to meet me." She slides her phone back into her pocket. "Just my luck."

"Want to come play a game while you wait for them?" I ask. Hey, nothing ventured nothing gained. She's definitely my type, but I don't know if I'm hers. My gaydar sucks, especially with other women.

"I don't think they're coming," she says. "Assholes. And I wasted all this time and money for nothing."

"Hang around for a bit, make the admission worthwhile. If I win a stuffed animal, it's all yours." I step forward and hold out my hand. "I'm Sabrina."

She smiles at me again, her features brightening. "Sonya." She takes my hand. It's dry, warm; both of mine are a bit damp from the heat. But she doesn't seem to mind. Our touch lingers a bit long, and I swear her gaze heats as she gives me a once-over. I feel a bit of a chill. A delicious chill.

"Which game is your favourite?"

Sonya looks around, spots a nearby tent. "Can you fish?"

"As long as we don't have to eat."

"Not these fish." Sonya laughs. "This will be way better than just going home."

"Of course it will. Remember, if I win a game, you can choose the stuffie."

We both laugh and head over to the tent. "We can't suck too badly at this, can we?"

"How hard can it be?"

Too fucking hard. The fish are different colours and the ones with any value are few and far between and hard to reach unless your arms are four feet long. Our poles cross as Sonya tracks a fish, her arm resting on mine, and I love the play of olive against dark chocolate. Thoughts of our legs entwined dance in my imagination. We try and we try, laughing, cursing, and it feels like I've known her for ages somehow.

"Get that one, there!" Sonya exclaims. I jerk towards the red fish, the one that would win me the biggest stuffed animal. And I miss. Dammit.

"It'll come around again," Sonya says. "Oh—wait..." She leans her fishing pole towards one of the blue fish. There are a few more of those. The water is populated with little yellow fish, their mouths gaping. But those won't get us much of anything.

"Yes!" The little blue fish closes its mouth around her bait and Sonya tugs it up and out.

The carnie comes over, taking the pole and fish from her. "You've got a choice of those stuffed animals there." He gestures to the one side, where some mid-sized, cheap-looking stuffed animals hang, forlornly. I doubt any of them are worth what we paid for the game itself.

Sonya studies the stuffed animals, finally reaching for a black and white penguin with a crazy mohawk in blue. "What do you think, Sabrina? What should I name him?" She bops my nose with the penguin's beak and makes a smooching sound. It's silly, but it does something to me. What if it were her lips instead?

"Bert? Like the guy in Mary Poppins?" I look back to the fish, spotting the red one coming around once more. I hold my pole out with its little plastic bait, aiming the best I can. The fish's mouth gapes and I drop the bait in, waiting for its mouth to close. It does, but only part way. Worth a shot. I gently jerk the line upwards, and the fish comes with the bait, just long enough for it to come out of the tray. But it doesn't stay. It falls to the ground.

"Sorry, try again," the carnie says, shrugging.

"Oh, come on," Sonya says. "She had that one. You owe her the big stuffed animal."

"Nope, I sure don't. It didn't stay. That's the rules."

Sonya puts her hands on her hips, and she looks fierce. "That's a rip-off."

"Tough luck." He takes my pole.

Sonya gives him a glare, but he rolls his eyes.

"It's not worth it," I say, putting my arm over Sonya's shoulders. "We'll try something else."

To my surprise, Sonya snuggles in against me as we walk away, heading down the concourse. "I have an idea," she says. I glance at her, and find her looking at me, her gaze intense. Those lips she licks are luscious. Oh to have a taste. But I'm still not sure.

Sonya tugs me between two tents, where we're somewhat out of view. It's getting darker, and it's darker still where we are. "I don't know about you, but I feel like this was fate."

It's a line, but it's not one I'm not going to reject. I lick my lips. "You're sure?"

Sonya wraps her arms around my neck. "I'll have to thank my friends for never showing up."

I lift my head and her lips are on mine, a light brush that turns into a deep, deep crush of mouths and tongues. It's just her and me, everything else fading to the background. It doesn't seem real, somehow, like I've been dreaming it, wishful thinking and all. But her warmth is right here, the poky nose of Bert the penguin resting against my shoulder. The heat of the sun still beats down on us. I don't want this to end.

"Oy! You two! Get a room!"

We break apart, and I look over at a group of teenage boys, gawking and pointing.

Sonya flips them the bird, and they laugh, but move on.

"Jerks," I mutter.

"Forget them." Sonya keeps me close, kissing my nose. "Can I buy you dinner?"

"As long as it's not scorpion pizza."

"Guaranteed. We can go somewhere, or there's always my place." She points to one of the high-rise condos a few blocks away. "That one's mine."

Maybe it is fate.

"That one's mine too."

"Fate," Sonya says. "Your place or mine?"

All I want is to see those Fluevogs on the floor. I can see them already, on my dark laminate by the bed.

"Mine."

ALYSSA LINN PALMER *writes romantic noir, lesbian romance, and a variety of short stories. Her novel* Betting on Love *was a finalist for a Rainbow Award in 2015, and in 2016, her novel* Midnight at the Orpheus *won a Rainbow Award for Best Bisexual Fiction. Find her works at alyssalinnpalmer.com, and all the usual online retailers. Want to chat? She's on Instagram and Twitter as @alyslinn, and on Facebook as herself.*

SOUNDTRACK
"These Boots Are Made For Walkin'" by Nancy Sinatra
"Let's Dance," by John Fluevog Shoes

VOYEUR

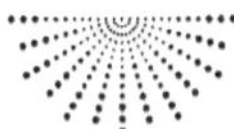

DIRK VAN DYK

*H*e enjoyed watching the revelry before joining the throbbing mass. Taking in all of the energy gave him a high, and voyeurism was an experience he appreciated. So was performance. He had chosen a higher vantage point, leaning casually on the railing above the dance floor. This gathering of queers was truly the greatest outdoor show on earth, and this dance floor was soon to be crowded with more sweaty bodies than the stage of the grandstand show. The night was full of possibility.

As he stood surveying the crowd, someone immediately commanded his attention. Yes. That one. Amidst the denim, glitter, and rhinestones—confidently wearing a cowboy hat and very little else. The smooth black leather caressing and framing his bare ass was delicious. Every toned muscle stood out from the tightness of the material pressing directly against skin. Firm, slightly squared, with soft downy hair gracing its countenance.

He imagined himself partaking of its pleasures, with a thrusting tongue, wet cum-laden fingers.

His cock piqued at the very thought of it. His eyes roamed down the chaps, around strong legs, to the boots. Beautifully crafted black and red leather cowboy boots with metal accents, gleaming as the occasional spotlight passed over them in the dusky, ever-more crowded rooftop. He could tell that the boots were well-worn and well-cared for. The creases had been kept supple, the metal polished, showing an investment in attention to detail. Care over time. He allowed himself to imagine the feeling of the leather against his own skin. His own body being massaged and cared for. He momentarily lost track of the scene before him.

He felt his groin strain towards the slightly rough material of his kilt, reminding him of the time when he first discovered that wearing a skirt could be sanctioned as a masculine act. The first time he had seen another queer like himself was in Montreal, effortlessly pulling off a marvellously messy head of hair and piercings wherever it pleased him, without rhyme or reason, a simple t-shirt, Doc Marten boots, and a utilikilt. The experience had left an indelible mark on him of what was possible. Confidence is incredibly sexy when it is genuine, and seasoned with the experience of conscientiously getting to know your body.

Queer bodies are rarely taken for granted.

Hard won, so to speak.

With a smile on his face, he returned to his own body, thick with moisture from the combination of rain and summer heat. It was getting darker, with the patio lights now glinting like fireflies against the city sky. The dance floor was fully packed now, and he could see the beautiful chaos of the Stampede grounds from his perch. Lights swirled in all directions on rides for those craving adventure through shifting their equilibrium, screaming with terrified delight. The lights left transient marks of colour across the sky as testaments to their ephemeral existences.

He knew these feelings, the craving for somatic sensation, pushing boundaries. He sunk into them every time he allowed a lover to tighten the screws on his clamps just a little bit more at his bidding. Metal and flesh becoming one. Consent and trust at the very core between two people. Exquisite ecstasy, ultimate control, painful pleasures. Catching each breath.

Rhythms of a different kind came back into his awareness. The music urged him to join the sparkling, joyous, wildly expressive rainbow of humanity before him. Such beauty in all that diversity. Walking down the few stairs toward the beating music, he caught sight of his chapped cowboy loitering near the edge of the crowd. As he appraised the muscle and girth beneath the leather harnesses across a wide chest and the shine of the metal rings against unshorn flesh, he looked up to see a direct and inviting appraisal in his own direction.

Approval.

Who had been watching whom?

DIRK VAN DYK *is a genderqueer writer, feminist, performer, educator, and artist inhabiting Treaty 7 and Metis Region 3 territories in Calgary, Alberta. They hold a Bachelor of Fine*

Arts, followed by other school adventures that allow space for creative projects, quiet reading, and taking in noble beasts.

SOUNDTRACK
"Erotica" by Madonna

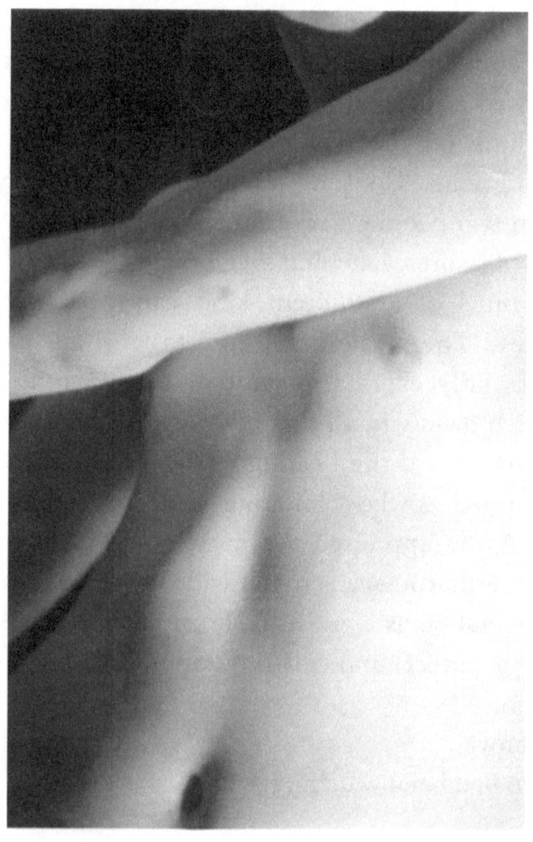

"Pose," Photograph by Shannon MacKinnon

ON THE RANGE

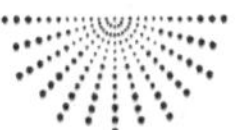

BY DALLAS BARNES

*W*hile my fellow Calgarians reminisce about childhoods filled with cotton candy, cowboy hats, candy apples, and cruelty to animals, I often compare my childhood in B.C. with those of my cowpeople counterparts. Although I have no idea what it was like to wear Wranglers and thick plaid shirts (insert lesbian stereotype joke here) in the glaring summer heat, I do know a few things about trying to be a lonely hero on the range.

I am a descendant of the great American dream. My forefolks rode proud on horses and the odd mule on the great Texas plains. They say all things are bigger in Texas and my sharers of DNA were no exception.

I rode proud on my purple glitter Sears Spyder bike with the striped banana seat, tasseled handlebars, and white wicker basket. They don't say all things are bigger in North Vancouver, but I was under the assumption that my neighbourhood was the centre of the universe and Texas had nothing on me.

Like the British, or the rattlesnakes, or the Mexicans who were pissed off at the Texans for stealing their land, I too had a thorn in my side of the great North Vancouver dream of freedom and geographical domination. His name was Wade and he was my little brother.

It was 1981, and my style, according to me, the eight year-old baby dyke, was a dead ringer for Kate Jackson's character in *Charlie's Angels*. In reality, I was a chunky Velma from *Scooby Doo*, except I wore my brown corduroy bell bottoms and my baby blue t-shirt with a full scale picture of the Dallas Cowboy Cheerleaders on it. I still don't know where I got the shirt, nor do I know why it was cool for an eight year-old to showcase the nearly not-dressed big-boobed and beautiful spectacle for the male gaze on her beans-and wieners-filled protruding belly—but I did—so, yeah.

My style and my bike were the perfect complement to July of 1981 in North Vancouver. On that particular morning, I woke up with aspirations of riding my freshly washed Sears Spyder and testing out the perfectly constructed chalk-drawn roadway I had meticulously drawn the day before. But, first things first—food. No good things are completed without a full belly.

My mom was on the couch with her legs curled underneath her. Her cigarette was burning, sitting in one of those little grooves in the 100-pound glass ashtrays they used to make. Her coffee was barely touched.

"Can I have Cheerios for breakfast?" I asked, adjusting the wedgy that happened every time I wore that 100 per cent polyester, floor-length, seafoam green nighty from Zellers. Somehow the static accumulated throughout the night seemed to concentrate in my ass.

"I guess," she said while looking through her coupon container in anticipation of her grocery shopping trip that day. "Don't make a mess, and see what your brother wants."

Ugh. Of course, I had to find out what my brother wanted. Wade, in my eyes, was only born to make my life miserable. He was the Gargamel to my Papa Smurf, the Ghost to my Pac-Man. My barrier in life, disguised as my younger brother.

I walked past his room, which smelled of old food and pee. He was sitting on his bed, sucking his thumb, staring blankly at his X-Wing Fighter poster.

"Mom wants to know what you want for breakfast."

"I want toast."

"Then you should make some."

"I'm not allowed"

"Because you're dumb."

"I'm telling Mom."

"Go ahead, I don't care."

"Maaaaaaaaaammmmmmmm! Dallas called me dumb!"

"Dallas, don't call your brother dumb."

Typical, I thought as I made my brother toast.

After breakfast, I brushed my teeth and ran to my room to find my Dallas Cowboy Cheerleaders shirt. I found it crumpled next to my bed, cheerleader boobs embedded in the mud accumulated on the bottoms of the corduroy bell bottoms from all the hard work I had done the day before.

"I am going out to play," I said as I struggled to fit my white wooden clogs over my thick white socks.

"Not until you clean your room." Mom's voice.

"My room is clean!" My protest.

"Ha! It's a pig-sty!"

"Maaaammmmm... can't I clean it when I get home?"

"No. Now. You told me you would do it this weekend."

Knowing that I had lost the battle, as I always did, I threw my clogs against the wall and ran to my room. I slammed the door.

"Don't slam your door."

Ugh. I can't win.

I quickly threw all of my toys in the closet. I made my bed. I ran a sticky Kool-Aid encrusted plastic cup to the kitchen. I was done.

I threw my clogs back on. "K, I'm going out to play."

"Take your brother with you."

"What? I hate taking him, he always cries." He did really cry a lot. It was embarrassing.

"You don't spend enough time with him. He is your brother for crying out loud."

"He's stupid, that's why I don't play with him."

"Dallas!"

"Mom!"

"Don't be smart."

"OK, I will be dumb then."

"Take him or you are not going out."

"Fine, but if I lose all of my friends because of him, it's your fault!"

I threw off my clogs and hit the same spot on the wall. I went to Wade's room to get him. He was sitting on his bed with his thumb in his mouth crying. Of course. I felt a little bad. But I didn't know why.

"Mom wants you to go out and play with me."

"You hate me."

"Oh my God. Just come outside."

He wiped his nose with his threadbare yellow blankie and stood up. He was still in his Snoopy pajamas.

"Mom, he is still in his pajamas!"

"Wade, put your clothes on and brush your teeth."

"I don't want to go outside with dumbhead."

"Fine, stay home then."

Unbelievable.

I once again put on my clogs. "I am going outside now."

"Not until you clean the mark on the wall where you threw your clogs."

Seriously?

I flipped off the clogs, again, with the might of a thousand wild horses. I made sure to hit the exact same spot on the wall that I was forced to clean up. I cleaned it off and went to the laundry room to throw the cloth in the washing machine and to my annoyance Wade was standing in front of the door.

"It's raining."

"Shut up."

"Dallas, you'd better put on your coat when you leave! It's pouring!" yelled my mom from the couch.

Clogs were thrown on with wild intention, coat forgotten. I ran out the door, slamming it behind me. My Spyder was, although gloriously purple and shiny, soaked in the sudden downpour Vancouver was known for.

I saddled up on the lustrous banana seat, hooked my clogs into the well-worn pedals and raced to my chalk-drawn roadway.

The roadway that was now a puddle of pink chalk particles.

I was no stranger to potential defeat, and I was no quitter. I saddled back on the Spyder, made sure my clogs were securely placed on the pedals and rode off in the North Vancouver rain, a lonely hero in the urban range.

I would recreate my roadway again the next day. Maybe I would let Wade help.

Maybe. Even lonely heroes need a sidekick, sometimes.

DALLAS BARNES *is a queer, cisgender, feminist, activist, and writer. She writes about life — its downfalls, turmoils, hilarities, and elations. Her experience with mental illness and all things queer makes her writing real, raw, and in your face. Dallas lives in Calgary, Alberta, with her cat Grizzly and tweets as @salladsenrab.*

SOUNDTRACK
"I Want to Break Free" by Queen

Photograph by Leslie Pringle

COMING

PW ZELLIE

y dirty cowboy sauntered across the corral, riding crop in hand. The sun was still 10 minutes from setting, so any neighbours driving down the isolated dirt road past the ranch may or may not realize that one of the long shadows being cast across the yard was not actually from the posts of the riding pen.

I shivered, my naked skin prickling, shivering, partly from the increasingly cool air, but mostly because I knew once she reached me, I would feel the caress of either her hand, or the sting of the crop. Part of me wanted to run, but I had given up that freedom when I had agreed to be tied to the cross-rail.

The pace of her stride slowed as she neared. I waited.

She could come.

And then so would I.

Cleverly disguised as a middle-aged nondescript librarian type, **PW ZELLIE** *glides through life, unremarked upon but grinning slyly, enjoying all life's yummy secrets.*

SOUNDTRACK
"Master & Servant" by Depeche Mode

Photograph by Leslie Pringle

THE STEWARD OF THE TREATY 7 SODIUM FOREST

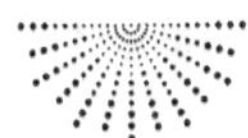

BY BEATRICE AUCOIN

July 6, 2532

I knew Uncle Danny was dead before I opened my eyes. I couldn't hear the raspy gasps that had punctuated his every breath since his cancer had started resisting all the treatments the matrices printer could give.

Uncle Danny had asked me yesterday to set up hammocks atop his favourite sodium tree. It stood slightly taller than its gleaming grey and white fellows beside the Elbow Arroyo and provided a view to the western mountains. The Old Earth Treaty 7 maps showed that this tree's location had been where the annual Stampede was last held about four hundred years ago. This city in Treaty 7 had about four million people at its height as a centre for climate change refugees.

Now I was the only person left.

"Why does it matter what used to be here?" I had once asked Uncle Danny when I was twelve years old. He had insisted I learn about Old Earth humans, as well as about building and repairing sodium trees.

He'd been a giant to me then. I remember his green eyes crinkling as he knelt down in front of me so we were eye level. I remember how I'd sometimes catch our reflections in the polished tree surfaces and see how the same yet different we were: long brown hair, tawny brown skin, husky 200-centimetre man; slender girl, then young woman who would end up boasting all of 157 centimetres in height.

"Because, Taiga, part of being a tree steward is knowing the story of the land and its people—good, bad, everything—so you know why we work for our civilization's survival."

I took in a shaky breath before I opened my eyes to look across at Uncle Danny in his hammock. He looked for all the world's carbon like he was sleeping.

I don't remember leaving to get the anti-grav and burial pod in the pre-dawn light, but I must have because suddenly the anti-grav had placed Uncle Danny inside the pod.

"Thank you," I whispered, holding his cold hand. "Thank you for everything. I love you."

If I'd had my way, I would have had dozens of people here from all over the Treaty Lands to mourn my uncle, a man who spent his life caring for the Treaty 7 sodium forest. This forest was part of the larger effort to undo humanity's climate change damage to the planet. The trees processed carbon and produced sodium bicarbonate that Uncle Danny and I would then stockpile for the autotrains to take to the Treaty 6 Lands.

If I'd had my way, I would have stayed longer with my

uncle's body to mourn, but I couldn't. The temperature was starting to rise; soon, it'd be too hot for me to be safe anywhere other than below the canopy.

I wondered if my friend Cano had heard Uncle Danny was dying. Even if they had, there was no way they could get here soon. Burial needed to be immediate because Uncle Danny had wanted to be placed inside a sodium tree, and the only hatches large enough for a burial pod were above the canopy. So I opened a hatch on the tree and had the anti-grav place Uncle Danny inside so he'd be in view of the mountains.

September 5, 2532

The temperature above the canopy was now too hot even before dawn to visit Uncle Danny's grave, so I was making sure to spend at least a few hours daily partaking in Old Earth history and culture because I knew that would have made my uncle happy.

I was also trying not to ruminate on the Central Treaties Government's lack of appropriate response.

I AM DYING STOP SEND MY NIECE HELP STOP STEWARD DANIEL EVERGREEN STOP

My uncle had sent that telegram not long before he died. He'd wanted help for *me*, not even thinking of himself.

Some nameless person in the more temperate region of Treaty II replied with the following days later.

CARBON PROCESSOR INSPECTOR ARRIVING AFTER HOT SEASON STOP

I had sent a telegram informing the government of Uncle Danny's death; there was no response.

A slight rumble told me the week's autotrain had arrived and was nestled in the Treaty 7 station in what was once the old city's downtown core. No one was on board the autotrain, of course, so I was in no rush to get there. The anti-gravs would load the sodium bicarbonate during the afternoon. My job then would be to check that the cars were properly loaded and sealed before the auto-train whooshed away.

That's why I took a short tumble out of the tree I was repairing when I heard a familiar tenor voice call out, "Taiga?"

In hindsight, I wish I had been wearing something other than bland grey coveralls. My hair was in a greasy topknot: when did I last wash it? And I had been loudly rapping along with and dancing in place to one of Uncle Danny's favourite Old Earth songs: "Tubthumping" by Chumbawamba.

Fortunately, I had been on a platform close to the ground, and a pair of strong arms caught my fall. I simply stared at the beautiful face in front of mine: light skin with a smattering of freckles across the cheeks, sky blue eyes, and brown hair pulled back into a ponytail.

The blue eyes stared back at me. Then the strong arms placed me gently on the ground. "I'm sorry I star-tled you!" Cano exclaimed. "Are you all right?"

"Hi!" I squeaked. What was the matter with me? Cano was an adorable, sexy human around my age, and my cognitive processes warped. That's the way it had been since I realized several years ago how much I really liked Cano. "Just not expecting anyone. How did you get here? Now, during the hot season?"

"I outfitted one of the autotrain cars to accommodate passengers," Cano said. "It stays cool enough to travel anytime. It's never made sense to me to have an inspector who can't travel for part of the year."

"You're the new carbon processor inspector?" I squealed. "Congratulations!"

They grinned, and my heart melted. "When my step-parent retired, I took over from them. I enjoy travelling the Treaty Lands, and my first stop was always going to be here." Cano suddenly stopped speaking and breathed in unsteadily. "I'm sorry about Danny; I only just found out. He was such a great guy."

A lump formed in my throat. "Thank you," I whispered.

"Would you like a hug?" Cano asked kindly.

I don't know how long I stayed there in their arms. I just know I didn't want to leave.

In case there were opportunities for more hugs—or other types of contact—I decided to have a shower. I wrapped my wet hair in a bun and dressed in an oversized green shirt and black leggings—note to self: have matrices printer make me some pretty clothes that show off my figure better—before joining Cano for lunch in my living quarters.

They told me all about how they had outfitted the autotrain car as a comfortable living space.

"I would love to see it if you don't mind," I said.

"Actually," they paused, "I was hoping to take you out to the desert this evening. There's a skyroof, and we can watch the stars if you want."

I reached over and squeezed Cano's hand. "Yes."

It was a while before we did any stargazing that night. When Cano and I finally turned our attention to the stars, we were wrapped in each other's arms and covered in naught but a blanket.

"Are you happy here?" they asked.

"Right now? Absolutely," I replied. "I was just happy several times, in fact."

They chuckled. "Well, I'm glad to hear that, but I mean in general. Do you want to be a sodium tree steward here?"

I looked up at the stars. "I love Treaty 7. It's my home. But I don't want to be alone anymore."

"What do you want, then?" Cano's voice was a gentle whisper.

"I'd like to teach others how to be tree stewards," I said. Just like Uncle Danny had taught me. "We might be scattered across the Treaty Lands, but we shouldn't have to be alone if we don't want to be."

"I agree," they said. "Let's figure out together how to bring people here to learn from and help you." Their arms tightened around me. "I won't leave for my next stop until there is at least one other person here. And I'd like to come visit you as often as I can."

"I've liked you for a long time, you know," I said.

"Me too," Cano replied. "You're amazing." They kissed my forehead then nestled against me.

I fell asleep listening to their heartbeat; I felt contented for the first time in what seemed like forever because I knew Cano would be here when I woke up.

BEATRICE AUCOIN *is a queer writer originally from Cape Breton. She makes her home in downtown Calgary with her wife, Brett Bergie; their son, Sam; and rescue cat, Tom. You can learn more about Beatrice's writing and cat sitting business at beatriceaucoin.com.*

SOUNDTRACK
"Tubthumping" by Chumbawamba

Photograph by Leslie Pringle

HAWK'S EYE

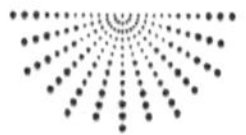

BY KAREN O.

I shift uncomfortably on my chair outside the corner coffee shop, and wait with a mixture of hope and apprehension while my date steps inside to place our order. The evening is warm, warmer than it should be even in July. There's a trickle of sweat on my forehead, and I wipe it with my fingertips. I cross my legs, smooth my skirt, and touch the polished Hawk's Eye pendant hanging from a delicate silver chain around my neck. I've loved its deep, mysterious darkness from the moment I saw it at the craft fair last spring, the way it drew in the light and begrudgingly released it again in bands of unnameable deepest blues. I had listened politely as the artisan described its mystical properties, how the stone could soothe distressed emotions and how it could help the soul be honest and find the courage to speak truth. The skeptic in me refuses to believe that an inanimate object, enchanting though it may be, can hold power over nature and emotions but tonight, I suspend disbelief and hope it is possible. Tonight, I need something to calm my anxiety, and I need the courage to speak truth.

Maybe this one will work out. It's going well, so far. I know it's only the third date and I still don't know him well but he seems like a good person. The way he stopped to give some change to that homeless man on 17th Avenue the other night—he didn't just toss some coins, he bent over and placed them in the man's hand, and he spent a minute chatting with him. Most people just walk past the homeless and look right through them like they're not there, but he treated him like a real person. That's someone I can get close to. It's just that…

"Here you go." Craig is back with the drinks and places our iced cappuccinos on the slatted tabletop, then sits down opposite me. He looks in my eyes and smiles, then his eyes drift downwards to the pendant, nestled in the V of my T-shirt, between the barely concealed swell of my breasts. He brings his eyes upwards again, embarrassed that I noticed, looks at me again and smiles, tiny wrinkles spreading out from the corners of his eyes. Laugh lines. A genuine smile shows the laugh lines. *He really must be happy to be with me.* I look at his eyes, and they're like the Hawk's Eye, bringing in the light but holding it, changing it, then letting it go in a fascinating, almost erotic manner. It's hard to look away. *Don't look too long, don't get drawn in, you could get hurt. Don't get too close yet. Not yet, not until after he knows. And maybe not even then.*

We're chatting as new acquaintances do, getting to know one another a little better, but I'm having trouble focusing now, fascinated by his muscular biceps and sinewy forearms, and by the light glinting golden off several days' growth of beard. Why do men do that, leaving it like that? Does he have any idea how much that turns me on? I barely know him but looking at him now... the things I want to do to him, the things I want him to do to me... But I can't go there; I have to stop thinking like this. I have to tell him about me. I should have told him on the second date. But I just wanted a bit more time, so he could get to know me—the me who I am aside from that other thing, so I'm not just someone with a label, so he knows me as a real person. Then maybe we can be together.

"Hmm? I'm sorry, I guess I wasn't listening. I've had something on my mind lately."

Here goes.

"Craig, there's something..."

Shit. That look. He's worried. Does he think I'm going to say I love him or something? Or maybe that I'm going to tell him this is our last date, that we're not a good match?

"Well, what is it?"

Now that creepy guy at the next table is listening. His eyes might be looking at his phone but his ears are aimed at me.

"It's nothing, really. You're finished your drink, why don't we go for a walk?"

The sun is just down, the western sky is giving up the day in slowly fading orange and yellow, blending upward to deepest blue overhead. Warm skylight softly surrounds and illuminates every building, every tree, every person. The magic hour, photographers call it, and the magic hour makes Craig look absolutely gorgeous.

His hand brushes slightly against my hand as we

walk. Is that an accident? A second time and I let him take mine in his. I shouldn't do this, but it feels good. It's been so long since I've felt affection from another person. I look up at him and smile. This feels good, and hopeful, but dangerous, too. We cross the street, wander into the park, music from the bandstand at the other end drifting down to us on the sultry evening air.

The Hawk's Eye pendant, warm against my skin, reminds me of what I must do but I don't want this to end; I don't want to tell him yet. I promise myself I'll tell him on the next date, if there is one. There must be one, why would he be holding my hand if he didn't like me, and didn't want to keep seeing me?

This end of the park is almost empty. No one else is near. I know I should tell him now, where there's privacy but still a degree of safety, just in case. Suddenly, he pulls me around to face him, and looks at me with those irresistibly inviting eyes. My hands are suddenly clammy, my heart is pounding—then his arms are around me, his lips are close, so close. I close my eyes as our lips touch and I give in to impulses I haven't felt in years.

"No, stop." I push him away, and he stands awkwardly, looking confused and hurt.

"What's wrong? I'm sorry, I didn't mean to upset you, I thought you wanted..."

"I did. I do. But I can't. Not yet. It's not right. You have to know something. It shouldn't matter, but it might. It matters to a lot of people and I'm tired of having to explain myself but I like you and I have to be honest. I'm transgender and it shouldn't matter, but there it is."

"Fuck. You're a goddam tra... Fuck!" He stands, staring silently, fists clenching, unclenching, clenching, then wheels around and strides away, towards the bandstand. Other people. Away from me.

I turn the other way, away from the bandstand, away from the people. Tears are going to come, and don't want anyone to see. I don't want anyone's sympathy. I just want to get away and be alone. I take a few steps to the curb, look down at the gutter and the drainage grate at my feet. I touch the Hawk's Eye, hold it in my hand, twist and pull, breaking the silver chain. In the twilight now, the stone is utterly black. I hold it for a moment, then let it slide through my fingers. It drops through the grate, into the darkness below, and I walk away into the darkening summer night.

KAREN O. *is puzzling out her future after leaving her last paying job but passes her time volunteering in the queer community, hiking in the mountains, and dabbling in writing. She is the T in LGBTQ and currently makes her home in Calgary.*

SOUNDTRACK
"I Will Survive" by Gloria Gaynor

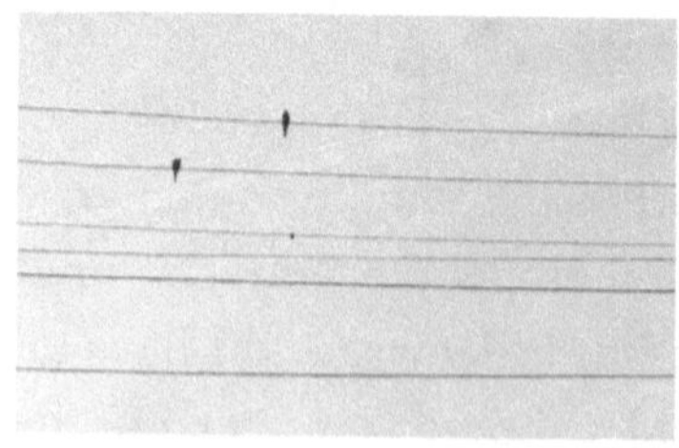

Photograph by Callan Field

AFTER CARE

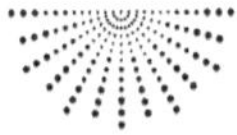

T

*L*ate afternoon. One of my tall brown chairs is pulled to the middle of the hardwood, as if on a stage. I am obediently draped over the seat, hair hanging to the floor with my naked ass in the air.

"These chairs are shorter than I thought," he says, from somewhere behind me. His thick hands fiddle with the yellow straps he works slowly, sweetly around my ankles and the chair legs. He is a perfectionist; wrapping and unwrapping me as he works me into whatever knots he fantasizes about.

"I'm just tall," I say to the floor, relaxing into my place. Trying not to cry; he still has to tie my wrists and I don't mean to ruin this. This sweet escape.

I lose myself on rough fingers and the sting of his palm on my ass. My pussy is dripping and I am crying for more, moaning, twisting, pulling lightly against my restraints. Pinned down and glad he can't see my face is dripping too. My emotions smudge lust and love and loss together: in the middle of riding roller coasters, I am riding grief and sorrow too.

When he is finished with me and I am satisfied a few times over, I go downstairs to get dressed. Naked in my closet I pull a leg through black panties and am suddenly overtaken by feeling. I am forced to sit down and finally let myself cry properly, raining hot tears and wracking sobs. Feeling that thing I didn't know I needed to feel.

"Babe?" He is at the closet door. He walks toward me as I palm at my eyes, looking up at him from the floor. And then my big, strong cowboy sits down and holds me. He wraps me up in his arms and legs, pulls me in and I rest my forehead on his bicep, naked and clinging to him while I let go. I have never been held like this before.

He makes me talk, just a little. Murmurs a few words into my hair. Is wiser than he gives himself credit for and suggests we cancel our plans and put on sweatpants.

Late evening. We are lying on my bed sheets in the loft, dark outside but it's a warm yellow here, just for us. I am the lucky recipient of his homemade chocolate straw-berries (the ones he promised would "wreck your diet" on his Tinder profile) and he is feeding me by hand.

We surprise ourselves with old-fashioned romance and fall in love.

T *is deep undercover, except when she bares all at boysboysboysandt.wordpress.com.*

SOUNDTRACK
S&M by Rhianna

FIRST RODEO

BY LOTIS CERVANTES

When I think of Stampede, I think of Chloe.

You see, I like Chloe but I'm what you can call in Filipino a *torpe*—a person who likes someone but couldn't make a move.

She was the first person I encountered when I was a temporary foreign worker at Tim Horton's.

When I came in, Chloe was pouring coffee but stopped to smile at me.

I smiled back.

No.

I smiled and then I stared.

Her hair was the colour of wheat and her eyes were as blue as the ocean while mine are brown and my short hair is dark as night.

Before I started drooling, I looked away then proceeded to the staff room to change.

Chloe was also nice.

I thought the only reason she was talking to me was because I was a novelty to her like the snow was to me—exciting... at first.

When I'd come in, she would be helping at the counter but would smile and say hi as soon as she saw me.

During breaks, she sat with me and asked questions about my family and why I moved to Canada.

I answered and tried to make eye contact but it was a struggle because I got distracted with how her eye colour changed from light to dark depending on her mood.

I stammered a lot and once she was gone, I criticized myself for being shy around her.

Because of these conversations, I began to think of Chloe more often than I should have.

The insane idea that I meant something to her too entered my mind.

But the truth was, I wasn't special like the seasonal donuts we offer.

Chloe talked to everyone.

She was a nice girl with an all-around Canadian charm and personality.

I came in one morning and heard her talking about Stampede.

She asked if I was going.

"To where?" I was as clueless as an empty coconut shell.

"Stampede."

"I don't know what that is."

She explained that it was "The Greatest Outdoor Show On Earth."

It lasted for a week and people dressed up in Western outfits.

"The celebration is at the Stampede grounds and you get to watch free concerts at the Coca-Cola stage, try the different rides, check out the exhibits and eat lots of food and mini-donuts." She smiled as she spoke, and she ended her explanation by asking if I would like to go with her and her friends.

I thought I heard the last part wrong so it took me a while to answer.

"It's okay if you don't want to. You probably have plans with your friends."

"No. I'll go with you..." I cleared my throat, "and your friends."

"Good." She smiled.

I reached the staff room walking on air.

At the last minute, she told me her friends couldn't make it because they had to work late.

"Do you want to cancel?" My heart sank when I said it.

"No. I really want to go now." My heart swelled.

"Okay."

We walked to Whitehorn Station and took the train to Victoria Park.

When we reached the grounds, I insisted on paying the entrance fee.

"I'll pay for the rides and food then."

Once we were inside, the park reminded me of the *peryahan* in the Philippines. A *peryahan* is similar to a travelling circus. They visit small towns during *fiestas* to set-up booths, rides and shows.

When I was a kid, I remember seeing a huge bill-board with the picture of a mermaid and a man who ate raw whole chickens.

The picture was poorly drawn, with one eye bigger than the other, faces that were angular and mouths wide enough to swallow misbehaving children and of course, raw whole chickens.

The artist used red and bold colours to express how horrifying the creatures were.

The drawing was effective. Passers-by would look at it and talk about going to the show.

I didn't see those billboards at the Stampede.

Chloe grabbed my hand and took me to the Midway.

We stood in front of a ride that shoots people up in the air and I felt nauseous just looking at it.

"Do you want to try it?" She pointed to the monstrosity.

"Sure." I swallowed.

She studied me and probably saw how pale I looked.

"Why don't we start with the Ferris Wheel?"

"Okay."

She paid for the ticket and we joined the long line.

She told me how she liked going to Stampede ever since she was a kid.

"Besides, the weather is so nice."

I didn't tell her that inside the red, long-sleeved plaid shirt I wore, I was sweating. I didn't understand why people would wear warm clothing in such sweltering heat.

When it was our turn to get in, she sat very close to me.

The edges of our hands were touching until I slowly withdrew mine.

She didn't notice how nervous I was sitting so close to her. I could smell the citrusy scent of her perfume.

By now, my infatuation had evolved into something deeper.

I really liked her but I don't know what to do with my feelings.

I had never been with a girl who wasn't a Filipina.

Also, I didn't want to misinterpret her niceness as something else.

I was afraid of being embarrassed, so I kept my feelings a secret.

If she noticed the stars in my eyes or how extra nervous I got when we were together, she didn't say anything.

But why would she?

I didn't even know if she's gay.

As the Ferris Wheel slowly rose up and we waited for the seats to be filled, I heard a country song blasting from the grounds.

"Do you like country music?" Chloe asked.

"Not really."

"What kind of music do you listen to?"

"Rock and alternative," I answered. "You?"

"Pop."

"Which pop artists do you like?"

"Ariana Grande, Selena Gomez, Taylor Swift." She grinned.

I felt so old all of a sudden but I was only twenty-six. Chloe was nineteen.

"Sing me a song." The Ferris Wheel rose higher till we could both see above the grounds and downtown Calgary.

"Why?"

"I heard Filipinos are really good singers." Her eyes twinkled, teasing me.

"I'm not sure I'm one of them."

"Come on." She tugged my sleeves. "We are not getting down from this ride until you sing to me."

"Well, aren't you demanding?" It was my turn to tease her and her cheeks turned red.

"Please?" She batted her long eyelashes and my heart careened like a bullet train.

"Okay, fine."

I cleared my throat and sang the first thing that came to mind.

"We watched the season pull up its own stage
And catch the last weekend of the last week
Before the gold and the glimmer have been
 replaced
Another sun soaked season fades away..."

I stopped.

Chloe clapped, her face lighting up with glee.

"See? You are good." She slapped my shoulder.

I shrugged, my face warm from the compliment.

The Ferris Wheel was big.

Chloe gripped the handlebars tight and when the wheel turned faster and faster, I saw that her eyes were closed.

"Are you okay?"

She shook her head and I noticed her legs were shaking as soon as we made our descent.

Without thinking, I took her hand and she held on to me tightly.

After the Ferris Wheel, we headed to the food stands where we bought a large box of pizza and pop.

We sat on the grass to eat and to people watch.

When we were done, she took me to a shooting range where I won a big brown teddy bear with a red heart on its chest.

She took me to the Indian Village to see real tepees.

We would have stayed to see the fireworks but she had to be home by ten.

Exhausted from the heat and the activities, the two of us were silent on the train.

I offered to walk her home and she refused at first but I insisted.

"This is me." We stopped in front of a brown bilevel house.

"Thank you for taking me to my very first Stampede."

"You're welcome." She smiled and was about to turn around when I called her name.

"Yes?"

"This is for you." I gave her the bear.

"But you won it."

"I know but I want you to have it."

"Are you sure?"

"Yes."

She took the bear and hugged it.

"Thank you."

I saluted and said goodbye but was only a few steps away when she called me back.

"Jennie?"

I turned around.

"Yes?"

"It was stolen, right?"

"What?" I frowned.

"The song? 'Stolen' by Dashboard Confessional?"

"Yes."

"You have stolen my heart."

"Yes. That's part of the lyrics."

"No."

"No?"

"You," Chloe pointed at me, "have stolen my heart." She pointed at the red heart on the bear's chest.

"Oh."

She tiptoed closer to me then kissed my lips.

LOTIS CLEMENTE CERVANTES *lives in Calgary with her wife. She is a yoga enthusiast (?) and a creator of LGBT-themed stories written in Taglish (Tagalog/English) that veer toward sadness/drama... which she claims is not intentional. She's the author of the novellas* Encore *and* Begin Again *(in English), and* Sequel Hearts: A Filipino LGBTQ Novel *(in Tagalog), available at all the usual places books are sold. You can also find her stories at Wattpad.com/lccervantes.*

SOUNDTRACK
"Stolen" by Dashboard Confessional
lyrics by Chris Carraba

Photograph by Leslie Pringle

YOU, AND THE HERDS

BY CALLAN FIELD

I was walking with my girlfriends when I saw you. We were on our way to Nashville North, with nothing more than a vague plan to slam shots and cowboys, although not necessarily in that order. The sun was setting, painting the sparse fair-weather clouds above us a mauve hue, and they had just turned on the fairground spotlights in response to the coming darkness. My eyes had been sailing across an ocean of leather boots, denim vests and straw hats when your midnight blue floral dress parted the Tacky Sea. Like Moses. You worked the spotlights as if you had walked the Milan runway a hundred times in those stilettos. As you did, the light caught the purple flowers on your dress, giving them the illusion of having just blossomed.

I was arrested by you.

Your red lipstick, thick chest hair and long nails pulled me in. But it was your eyes that held me firmer than the metal handcuffs permanently attached to the head of my bed. Later, when you ask, I'll tell you that the cuffs are indeed authentic. Your eyes were those of a green fire, one that offered a comfortable cremation.

I'd bet everything that you were a Slytherin.

You kept walking and my eyes followed while my body continued onwards into a bro-ring. Despite on-going education efforts and outreach, bro-rings remain a serious public health risk due to their regular appear-ances at large gatherings. I bumped into an unmoveable bro, dashing my fantasy that I qualified as an unstop-pable force. I panicked as I fell. My hands flailed towards Mr. Rat, first name Jim, missing his arms, and then his ass before tumbling down to his feet. I might have been able to find purchase on his derrière, had it not been willfully ignored and flatter than a Manitoba field.

As I lay coughing in the dirt, it struck me as tragic that I had planned to perform this stunt willingly at Nashville North in a desperate attempt at seduction. It may or may not have been a Stampede tradition, as much a staple as the rodeo.

My curtain call to my own rodeo came early.

My coughing turned to wheezing as my asthma kicked in.

I thought how happily I would trade all of those past attempts at unworthy men for a chance to touch your dress once. I revelled in the thought of combing through your closet, admiring each curated piece of your wardrobe, before pulling it off its wooden hangar and down onto my body. Seconds after having seen you, I ached for you. To be you. I saw myself spinning under the fairground lights, the world a blur but for the twirling hem of your dress keeping pace with me.

Mr. Rat stepped over me without a glance down, the

spur on his boots clicking on the concrete as he followed his herd northbound. My bitches were gone, and probably the migrations bait.

You would be gone too. I sighed in the dust, and wheezed some more.

A shadow was cast over me, and a hand, rough with callouses, was offered. It was yours. You pulled me up without exertion. Once vertical, I continued to hold your hand. I inspected the pink nails and the single turquoise opal annotating your ring finger. I could see a raven etched into the silver band.

"Thanks."

"It would be wise to exercise caution with that gaze."

Our eyes remained as locked as our hands.

"It may have gotten me into trouble before." I had the desire to wink.

I smiled slightly, you laughed, and I smiled wider.

"We're leaving," you said. I realized your friends ringed us, facing outwards like muskox.

"Where to?"

You shrugged, and started walking south before replying, "Home. Time for you to leave the zoo."

Our grip shifted, but neither of us let go.

CALLAN FIELD *is a queer Canadian artist, adventure(r) and dog lover – allergies be damned. An emerging visual artist, he studied environmental science before completing his BFA at Ryerson University in 2014. While his primary medium is* *photography, his work has expanded to include writing, video, and installation. He was recently selected for The Peel, a multi-layered project featuring six Canadian artists as they canoed into the Arctic Circle through the Peel River Watershed. The documentary and touring exhibition follows the journey of each artist as they express the experience through their unique medium. Learn more at thepeel.ca, and find out more about Callan at callanfield.com and @callanfield on Instagram.*

SOUNDTRACK
"Creep City" by Jake Shears

Photograph by Callan Field

DHAKIRA

BY M. JANE COLETTE

Sheesha. Smoke. Delicious. I inhale. Cough.

"I can't believe you brought me here."

She refuses to take the pipe. I shrug. Take another puff.

"Seriously. What were you thinking?"

She's pissed off, and I suppose I understand. The air outside is disgusting—Apocalypse Now, the globe is on fire, motherfuckers, as Bill Nye so eloquently put it. More than 500 summer fires raging in Northern Alberta, and a smoke blanket covering pretty much all of the 661,848 km² of the province.

"I figured, why not? We're all going to die of lung cancer at this point anyway," I say. Inhale. Hold it in my lungs for just a little longer than I ought to. Swallow. Exhale without coughing. "Anyway. This smoke—it's different. Magic. Sensual."

"It's not that." She's agitated and I try to pay attention to her, and not the pipe. Which is gorgeous and ornate, and probably hasn't been properly cleaned for years, and makes me homesick and happy all at the same time.

"What is it then?" I ask. Inhale.

"Do you want us to get beat up?" And she's really anxious. Angry. I don't get it. Look at her.

"What?"

"What were you thinking?" She looks around.

So do I. Through the smoke. I love it here: the ventilation is kinda shitty, so the smoke forms thick clouds in the air, hangs around awhile before disappearing. The green apple and gum mint flavours tickle my nostrils. The tables creak. The music is too loud, the voices, predominantly Arabic, but at that table, over there, that's Farsi.

"Do you want us to get beat up?" she says again. And the panic in her voice is real. I reach for a hand.

"What?"

"We are the only two lesbians here."

"You are the only lesbian here," I tease. Look around again, try to see the lounge through her eyes. "We are the only two women here. No—look, there are two over there."

"They're with men, not alone. What's wrong with you? This is not a safe space."

Is it not? I didn't think—I look around again. The men, from eighteen to eighty, are focused on themselves, their pipes, their tea, and their Barbican, not us. Nobody's looking.

I come here all the time.

"This is my safe space," I say. But suddenly, her fear infects me. Is it? Am I deluded?

"Are you blind?"

Sheesha. Smoke. Inhale. Exhale. Memories of souks and empty Mediterranean Sea beaches, Roman ruins, mandarin orchards. Oil-covered hedgehogs and Bedouin boys covered with dust. Barefoot dark-haired girls—their black-eyed, hennaed mothers—warm *habaz* from the bakery and cold Pepsi poured into plastic bags... but never Coke. Explaining the *ghibli* wind, and how to avoid centipedes and scorpions, to the new children. Sifting maggots with a colander out of a hard-won bag of rice. Gaddafi on the television screen, sounded muted. Santa Claus in *Jamahiriya* green.

Children remember the strangest things.

I am not blind, and this is my safe place.

"No. Not blind. But maybe sedated. Come on. Smoke."

She takes the pipe from me but does not raise it to her lips—holds it in her hands as she would a bong, and I laugh. She gives me a look. I devour it.

"This is the worst one yet," she says.

"You haven't tasted it. Yet." I reach for the pipe and bring it to her lips. She parts them, slowly.

"The worst place," she says. "Sheesha lounge after sheesha lounge you drag me to. This one? The worst one."

"The most phallic-centric one, perhaps," I tease. "Not the worst."

This is, actually, my favourite one. Divey, dirty, loud. The service is awful. The food, outrageously expensive—they don't actually want you to buy it, and this I know for a fact. That the clientele is all Middle Eastern men, the occasional woman in a *hijab*... well, that's not a downside for me. Early imprinting. Bedouin boys, dark-haired, black-eyed girls.

"You're so weird," my dark-haired girl, her eyes black with anger, says. I shrug. This, after all, is why she loves me. Sorta.

"I didn't think you'd go all goldstar lesbian on me because of all the cocks in the room." I'm teasing but also treading on dangerous ground. We may be lovers, we may be almost the same age—but we share no common story, and virtually no common experiences. Slavic girl raised in a foreign workers' camp in Libya, half-Arab girl from middle of nowhere Wonder Bread Saskatchewan. Our fears, our triggers—an ocean apart. Literally.

"Goldstar lesbian manhater," I murmur. Lean across the table so I can whisper in her ear. "Or are you just being a racist Muslim-hating bitch, ashamed of your Baba's heritage? Which is it?"

"Bisexual slut," she hisses out with the smoke and I am so happy she's finally smoking. The smoke is delicious and it soothes; her mood is changing. "This is where you come to pick up your boys?"

I've never ever picked up a man in a sheesha lounge —although once, a Brazilian movie actress, fuck yes, thank you, God. But I won't tell her how virtuous I usually am in sheesha lounges, not tonight. Tonight, I want her angry and on edge, and pushing and punishing me. Yes. Preferably in a public place.

"I've never picked up a dude in a sheesha lounge," I tell her. "But I've fucked a Persian boy in the toilet of one."

She flushes.

"Keeping your fucking voice down."

"And a Syrian one in an alley just a couple of blocks over. Just outside his apartment building—so turned on, we couldn't quite make it inside."

"What's wrong with you? Seriously?"

She's really pissed now. I've crossed the line, not funny, wrecked the mood.

I look away, suddenly crushed and mortified, and my safe place is not keeping me safe even though a heartrending voice is singing "Habibi" in the background.

I love her and I think she loves me, but nothing is ever simple, clear cut between us. Each of us speaks a foreign language, each of us is a foreign land. I find her difficult, hard to please, easy to offend—she finds me exhausting, unpredictable. Freaky, and not in a good way.

Why the fuck are we together?

I blow sheesha smoke in her face.

"What are you doing?"

"That's how they flirt in Colombia," I say.

"And now you're going to tell me about the Colombian boy you've fucked in the toilet of a taqueria?"

I've never ever fucked a Colombian boy. The taqueria —surely, I haven't told her *that* story?—that was also a Persian boy. But we won't go there, not tonight. And I won't tell her about the Colombian girl. That would maybe be the end.

The boys infuriate her; a girl, she would not forgive. I think it's weird; she says it's logical.

I give her a kick under a table.

"What?"

"Let's go find a taqueria."

"What's wrong with you?"

"Everything. Sheesha makes me horny. And you're

not having a good time here. Let's go somewhere else."

For a few seconds, I see her think about insisting that we stay—just because I suggested that we go. But then she nods.

She rests her hand on the nape of my neck as soon as we are out the door.

"And what was all that about, *habibti*?"

I could be demure. But I spoke the truth. Sheesha makes me horny. I take the hand that's not on my neck and, without pretense at foreplay, thrust it under my skirt.

"Bisexual slut," she whispers. Moves closer to me.

"If you fuck me in the doorway of the sheesha lounge, I will never ever be able to come back here, and this is my safe place," I tell her. "Do not ruin it for me, you racist manhating lesbian. Now. Taqueria?"

She grinds against me a little, her hand under my skirt and between us, my neck immobile in the vice of her grip.

"Is the restroom clean?" she asks.

I shake my head. "Filthy. It's fucking filthy."

She sighs. I inhale her. She's delicious.

"What's wrong with you?"

Everything.

But she loves it.

"Taqueria?" I ask.

M. JANE COLETTE *thinks the best fiction reads like truth and the best truth reads like fiction. Her published 'is it literature or is it porn' novels include* Tell Me, Consequences (of defensive adultery), Cherry Pie Cure, *and* Text Me, Cupid, *a (slightly) dirty love story for 21st century adults who don't believe in true love but want it anyway. She's also the author of the non-fiction collection of essays on language, taboos, and the business of writing, CUNT versus PUSSY (reissued in 2017 with the more library-friendly title Rough Draft Confessions). Connect with @mjanecolette on Twitter and Instagram or whisper secrets to her at TellMe@mjaneco-lette.com.*

SOUNDTRACK
"Sweet Dreams" by Eurythmics

Photograph by Leslie Pringle

Queer Summer Night in Cowtown is the fourth collaborative project by YYC Queer Writers, formed in 2013 by writer and activist Dallas Barnes. We get together intermittently to... write. Also, laud our lovers. Commiserate about our exes. Share what we wrote. Explain what we want to write. Try to justify why we aren't writing it. Go home and write it. Come back. Share it... repeat.

We believe telling and sharing stories is how we change the world.

In YYC and want to write with us? Find us on Facebook at Calgary Queer Writing Group or send us a note through *mjanecolette.com/yycqueerwriters*.

MORE PROJECTS

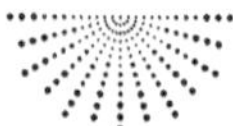

BY YYC QUEER WRITERS

- *Screw Chocolate: 14 QUEER valentines to get you through February 14*, February 2017
- *Queer Christmas in Cowtown*, December 2017
- *Screw Chocolate 2*, February 2018
- *Queer Christmas In Cowtown 2, Letters to Santa*, coming December 2019. Accepting submissions until September 22, 2019.

Interested in contributing? Go to *mjanecolette.com/ yycqueerwriters* for details.